HORRiD HENRY'S CHRiSTMAS CRACKER

Francesca Simon spent her childhood on the beach in California, and then went to Yale and Oxford Universities to study medieval history and literature. She now lives in London with her family. She has written over 50 books and won the Children's Book of the Year in 2008 at the Galaxy British Book Awards for *Horrid Henry and the Abominable Snowman*.

Also by Francesca Simon
Don't Cook Cinderella
Helping Hercules

For younger readers
Café at the Edge of the Moon
Mr P's Naughty Book
The Parent Swap Shop
Illustrated by Pete Williamson

Spider School
Illustrated by Tony Ross

Barnyard Hullabaloo
Billy the Kid Goes Wild
Chicks Just Want to Have Fun
Mish Mash Hash
Moo Baa Baa Quack
Runaway Duckling
Where are my Lambs?
The Haunted House of Buffin Street
Jogger's Big Adventure
Look at Me
Meet the Gang
Miaow Miaow Bow Wow
Rampage in Prince's Garden
Yum Yum
The Topsy Turvies
Illustrated by Emily Bolam

There is a complete list of **Horrid Henry** titles
at the end of the book.

Visit Horrid Henry's website at **www.horridhenry.co.uk** for
competitions, games, downloads and a monthly newsletter!

HORRiD HENRY'S
CHRISTMAS
CRACKER

Francesca Simon
Illustrated by Tony Ross

Orion
Children's Books

ORION CHILDREN'S BOOKS

First published in Great Britain in 2006 by Orion Children's Books
Reissued 2008 by Orion Children's Books
This edition published in 2015 by Hodder and Stoughton

9

A CIP catalogue record for this book
is available from the British Library.

ISBN 978 1 40723 046 7

Printed and bound in Great Britain by
Clays Ltd, St Ives plc

The paper and board used in this book are
made from wood from responsible sources.

Orion Children's Books
An imprint of
Hachette Children's Group
Part of Hodder & Stoughton
Carmelite House
50 Victoria Embankment
London EC4Y 0DZ

An Hachette UK Company
www.hachette.co.uk

www.hachettechildrens.co.uk
www.horridhenry.co.uk

For the one and only
Miranda Richardson

CONTENTS

HORRID HENRY'S CHRISTMAS PLAY

A cold dark day in November
(37 days till Christmas)

Horrid Henry slumped on the carpet and willed the clock to go faster. Only five more minutes to hometime! Already Henry could taste those crisps he'd be sneaking from the cupboard.

Miss Battle-Axe droned on about school dinners (yuck), the new drinking fountain blah blah blah, maths homework blah blah blah, the school Christmas play blah blah . . . what? Did Miss Battle-Axe

1

say . . . Christmas play? Horrid Henry sat up.

'This is a brand-new play with singing and dancing,' continued Miss Battle-Axe. 'And both the older and the younger children are taking part this year.'

Singing! Dancing! Showing off in front of the whole school! Years ago, when Henry was in the infants' class, he'd played eighth sheep in the nativity play and had snatched the baby from the manger and refused to hand him back. Henry hoped Miss Battle-Axe wouldn't remember.

Because Henry had to play the lead. He had to. Who else but Henry could be an all-singing, all-dancing Joseph?

'I want to be Mary,' shouted every girl in the class.

'I want to be a wise man!' shouted Rude Ralph.

'I want to be a sheep!' shouted Anxious Andrew.

'I want to be Joseph!' shouted Horrid Henry.

'No, me!' shouted Jazzy Jim.

'Me!' shouted Brainy Brian.

'Quiet!' shrieked Miss Battle-Axe. 'I'm the director, and my decision about who will act which part is final. I've cast the play as follows: Margaret. You will be Mary.' She handed her a thick script.

Moody Margaret whooped with joy. All the other girls glared at her.

'Susan, front legs of the donkey; Linda, hind legs; cows, Fiona and Clare. Blades of grass—' Miss Battle-Axe continued assigning parts.

Pick me for Joseph, pick me for Joseph, Horrid Henry begged silently. Who better than the best actor in the school to play the starring part?

'I'm a sheep, I'm a sheep, I'm a

3

beautiful sheep!' warbled Singing Soraya.

'I'm a shepherd!' beamed Jolly Josh.

'I'm an angel,' trilled Magic Martha.

'I'm a blade of grass,' sobbed Weepy William.

'Joseph will be played by—'

'ME!' screamed Henry.

'Me!' screamed New Nick, Greedy Graham, Dizzy Dave and Aerobic Al.

'—Peter,' said Miss Battle-Axe. 'From Miss Lovely's class.'

Horrid Henry felt as if he'd been slugged in the stomach. Perfect Peter?

4

His *younger* brother? Perfect Peter get the starring part?

'It's not fair!' howled Horrid Henry.

Miss Battle-Axe glared at him.

'Henry, you're—' Miss Battle-Axe consulted her list. Please not a blade of grass, please not a blade of grass, prayed Horrid Henry, shrinking. That would be just like Miss Battle-Axe, to humiliate him. Anything but that—

'—the innkeeper.'

The innkeeper! Horrid Henry sat up, beaming. How stupid he'd been: the *innkeeper* must be the starring part. Henry could see himself now, polishing glasses, throwing darts, pouring out big foaming Fizzywizz drinks to all his happy customers while singing a song about the joys of innkeeping. Then he'd get into a nice long argument about why there was no room at the inn, and finally, the chance to slam the door in Moody

5

Margaret's face after he'd pushed her away.
Wow. Maybe he'd even get a second song.
'Ten Green Bottles' would fit right into
the story: he'd sing and dance while
knocking his less talented classmates off
a wall. Wouldn't that be fun!

Miss Battle-Axe handed a page to
Henry. 'Your script,' she said.

Henry was puzzled. Surely there were
some pages missing?

He read:

(Joseph knocks. The innkeeper opens the door.)

JOSEPH: Is there any room at the inn?
INNKEEPER: No.

(The innkeeper shuts the door.)

Horrid Henry turned over the page.

It was blank. He held it up to the light.

There was no secret writing. That was it.

His entire part was one line. One stupid puny line. Not even a line, a word. 'No.'

Where was his song? Where was his dance with the bottles and the guests at the inn? How could he, Horrid Henry, the best actor in the class (and indeed, the world) be given just one word in the school play? Even the donkeys got a song.

Worse, after he said his *one* word, Perfect Peter and Moody Margaret got to yack for hours about mangers and wise men and shepherds and sheep, and then

7

sing a duet, while he, Henry, hung about behind the hay with the blades of grass.

It was so unfair!

He should be the star of the show, not his stupid worm of a brother. Why on earth was Peter cast as Joseph anyway? He was a terrible actor. He couldn't sing, he just squeaked like a squished toad. And why was Margaret playing Mary? Now she'd never stop bragging and swaggering.

AAARRRRGGGGHHHH!

'Isn't it exciting!' said Mum.

'Isn't it thrilling!' said Dad. 'Our little boy, the star of the show.'

'Well done, Peter,' said Mum.

'We're so proud of you,' said Dad.

Perfect Peter smiled modestly.

'Of course I'm not *really* the star,' he said, 'Everyone's important, even little parts like the blades of grass and the innkeeper.'

Horrid Henry pounced. He was a Great White shark lunging for the kill.

'AAAARRRRGGGHH!' squealed Peter. 'Henry bit me!'

'Henry! Don't be horrid!' snapped Mum.

'Henry! Go to your room!' snapped Dad.

Horrid Henry stomped upstairs and

9

slammed the door. How could he bear the humiliation of playing the innkeeper when Peter was the star? He'd just have to force Peter to switch roles with him. Henry was sure he could find a way to persuade Peter, but persuading Miss Battle-Axe was a different matter. Miss Battle-Axe had a mean, horrible way of never doing what Henry wanted.

Maybe he could trick Peter into leaving the show. Yes! And then nobly offer to replace him.

But unfortunately, there was no guarantee Miss Battle-Axe would give Henry Peter's role. She'd probably just replace Peter with Goody-Goody Gordon. He was stuck.

And then Horrid Henry had a brilliant, spectacular idea. Why hadn't he thought of this before? If he couldn't play a bigger part, he'd just have to make his part bigger. For instance, he could *scream* 'No.' *That* would get a reaction. Or he could bellow 'No,' and then hit Joseph. I'm an angry innkeeper, thought Horrid Henry, and I hate guests coming to my inn. Certainly smelly ones like Joseph. Or he could shout 'No!', hit Joseph, then rob him. I'm a robber innkeeper, thought Henry. Or, I'm a robber *pretending* to be an inn-keeper. That would liven up the play a bit. Maybe he could be a French robber innkeeper, shout '*Non*', and rob Mary and Joseph. Or he was a French robber *pirate* innkeeper, so he could shout '*Non*,' tie Mary and Joseph up and make them walk the plank. Hmmm, thought Horrid Henry. Maybe my

part won't be so small. After all,
the innkeeper *was* the most important
character.

12 December
(only 13 more days till Christmas)

Rehearsals had been going on forever.
Horrid Henry spent most of his time
slumping in a chair. He'd never seen such
a boring play. Naturally he'd done everything he could to improve it.

'Can't I add a dance?' asked
Henry.

'No,' snapped Miss
Battle-Axe.

'Can't I add a
teeny-weeny-little
song?' Henry pleaded.

'No!' said Miss
Battle-Axe.

'But how does the

innkeeper *know* there's no room?' said Henry. 'I think I should—'

Miss Battle-Axe glared at him with her red eyes.

'One more word from you, Henry, and you'll change places with Linda,' snapped Miss Battle-Axe. 'Blades of grass, let's try again . . .'

Eeek! An innkeeper with one word was infinitely better than being invisible as the hind legs of a donkey. Still—it was so unfair. He was only trying to help.

22 December
(only 3 more days till Christmas!)

Showtime! Not a teatowel was to be found in any local shop. Mums and dads had been up all night frantically sewing costumes. Now the waiting and the rehearsing were over.

Everyone lined up on stage behind the

curtain. Peter and Margaret waited on the side to make their big entrance as Mary and Joseph.

'Isn't it exciting, Henry, being in a real play?' whispered Peter.

'NO,' snarled Henry.

'Places, everyone, for the opening song,' hissed Miss Battle-Axe. 'Now remember, don't worry if you make a little mistake: just carry on and no one will notice.'

14

'But I still think I should have an argument with Mary and Joseph about whether there's room,' said Henry. 'Shouldn't I at least check to see—'

'No!' snapped Miss Battle-Axe, glaring at him. 'If I hear another peep from you, Henry, you will sit behind the bales of hay and Jim will play your part. Blades of grass! Line up with the donkeys! Sheep! Get ready to baaa . . . Bert! Are you a sheep or a blade of grass?'

'I dunno,' said Beefy Bert.

Mrs Oddbod went to the front of the stage. 'Welcome everyone, mums and dads, boys and girls, to our new Christmas play, a little different from previous years. We hope you all enjoy a brand new show!'

Miss Battle-Axe started the CD player. The music pealed. The curtain rose. The audience stamped and cheered. Stars twinkled. Cows mooed. Horses neighed. Sheep baa'ed. Cameras flashed.

Horrid Henry stood in the wings and watched the shepherds do their Highland dance. He still hadn't decided for sure how he was going to play his part. There were so many possibilities. It was so hard to choose.

Finally, Henry's big moment arrived.

He strode across the stage and waited behind the closed inn door for Mary and Joseph.

Knock!

Knock!
Knock!

The innkeeper stepped forward and opened the door. There was Moody Margaret, simpering away as Mary, and Perfect Peter looking full of himself as Joseph.

'Is there any room at the inn?' asked Joseph.

Good question, thought Horrid Henry. His mind was blank. He'd thought of so many great things he *could* say that what he was *supposed* to say had just gone straight out of his head.

'Is there any room at the inn?' repeated Joseph loudly.

'Yes,' said the innkeeper. 'Come on in.'

Joseph looked at Mary.

Mary looked at Joseph.

The audience murmured.

Oops, thought Horrid Henry. Now he remembered. He'd been supposed to say no. Oh well, in for a penny, in for a pound.

The innkeeper grabbed Mary and Joseph's sleeves and yanked them through the door. 'Come on in, I haven't got all day.'

' . . . but . . . but . . . the inn's *full*,' said Mary.

'No it isn't,' said the innkeeper.

'Is too.'

'Is not. It's my inn and I should know. This is the best inn in Bethlehem, we've got TVs and beds, and—' the innkeeper paused for a moment. What *did* inns have in them? '—and computers!'

Mary glared at the innkeeper.

The innkeeper glared at Mary.

Miss Battle-Axe gestured frantically from the wings.

'This inn looks full to me,' said Mary firmly. 'Come on Joseph, let's go to the stable.'

'Oh, don't go there, you'll get fleas,' said the innkeeper.

'So?' said Mary.

'I love fleas,' said Joseph weakly.

'And it's full of manure.'

'So are you,' snapped Mary.

'Don't be horrid, Mary,' said the innkeeper severely. 'Now sit down and

19

rest your weary bones and I'll sing you a song.' And the innkeeper started singing:

'Ten green bottles, standing on a wall
Ten green bottles, standing on a wall,
And if one green bottle should accidentally
   fall—'

'OOOHHH!' moaned Mary. 'I'm having the baby.'

'Can't you wait till I've finished my song?' snapped the inkeeper.

'NO!' bellowed Mary.

Miss Battle-Axe drew her hand across her throat.

Henry ignored her. After all, the show must go on.

'Come on, Joseph,' interrupted Mary. 'We're going to the stable.'

'OK,' said Joseph.

'You're making a big mistake,' said the innkeeper. 'We've got satellite TV and . . .'

Miss Battle-Axe ran on stage and nabbed him.

'Thank you, innkeeper, your other guests need you now,' said Miss Battle-Axe, grabbing him by the collar.

'Merry Christmas!' shrieked Horrid Henry as she yanked him off-stage.

There was a very long silence.

'Bravo!' yelled Moody Margaret's deaf aunt.

Mum and Dad weren't sure what to do. Should they clap, or run away to a place where no one knew them?

Mum clapped.

Dad hid his face in his hands.

'Do you think anyone noticed?' whispered Mum.

Dad looked at Mrs Oddbod's grim face. He sank down in his chair. Maybe one day he would learn how to make himself invisible.

'But what was I *supposed* to do?' said Horrid Henry afterwards in Mrs Oddbod's office. 'It's not *my* fault I forgot my line. Miss Battle-Axe said not to worry if we made a mistake and just to carry on.'

Could he help it if a star was born?

2

HORRID HENRY'S CHRISTMAS PRESENTS

23 December
(Just two more days to go!!!)

Horrid Henry sat by the Christmas tree and stuffed himself full of the special sweets he'd nicked from the special Christmas Day stash when Mum and Dad weren't looking. After his triumph in the school Christmas play, Horrid Henry was feeling delighted with himself and with the world.

Granny and Grandpa, his grown-up cousins Pimply Paul and Prissy Polly, and

their baby Vomiting Vera were coming
to spend Christmas. Whoopee, thought
Horrid Henry, because they'd all have
to bring *him* presents. Thankfully, Rich
Aunt Ruby and Stuck-Up Steve weren't
coming. They were off skiing. Henry
hadn't forgotten the dreadful lime green
cardigan Aunt Ruby had given him last
year. And much as he hated cousin Polly,
anyone was better than Stuck-Up Steve,
even someone who squealed all the
time and had a baby who threw up on
everyone.

Mum dashed into the sitting room,
wearing a flour-covered apron and
looking frantic. Henry choked down
his mouthful of sweets.

'Right, who wants to decorate the
tree?' said Mum. She held out a card-
board box brimming with tinsel and gold
and silver and blue baubles.

'Me!' said Henry.

'Me!' said Peter.

Horrid Henry dashed to the box and scooped up as many shiny ornaments as he could.

'I want to put on the gold baubles,' said Henry.

'I want to put on the tinsel,' said Peter.

'Keep away from my side of the tree,' hissed Henry.

'You don't have a side,' said Peter.

'Do too.'

'Do not,' said Peter.

'I want to put on the tinsel *and* the baubles,' said Henry.

'But I want to do the tinsel,' said Peter.

'Tough,' said Henry, draping Peter in tinsel.

'Muuum!' wailed Peter. 'Henry's hogging all the decorations! And he's putting tinsel on me.'

'Don't be horrid, Henry,' said Mum. 'Share with your brother.'

Peter carefully wrapped blue tinsel round the lower branches.

'Don't put it there,' said Henry, yanking it off. Trust Peter to ruin his beautiful plan.

'MUUUM!' wailed Peter.

'He's wrecking my design,' screeched Henry. 'He doesn't know how to decorate a tree.'

'But I wanted it there!' protested Peter. 'Leave my tinsel alone.'

'You leave my stuff alone then,' said Henry.

'He's wrecked my design!' shrieked Henry and Peter.

'Stop fighting, both of you!' shrieked Mum.

'He started it!' screamed Henry.

'Did not!'

'Did too!'

'That's enough,' said Mum. 'Now, whose turn is it to put the fairy on top?'

'I don't want to have that stupid fairy,' wailed Horrid Henry. 'I want to have Terminator Gladiator instead.'

'No,' said Peter. 'I want the fairy. We've always had the fairy.'

'Terminator!'

'Fairy!'

'TERMINATOR!'

'FAIRY!'

Slap Slap

'WAAAAAAA!'

'We're having the fairy,' said Mum firmly, 'and *I'll* put it on the tree.'

'NOOOOOO!' screamed Henry. 'Why can't we do what I want to do? I never get to have what I want.'

'Liar!' whimpered Peter.

'I've had enough of this,' said Mum. 'Now get your presents and put them under the tree.'

Peter ran off.

Henry stood still.

'Henry,' said Mum. 'Have you finished wrapping your Christmas presents?'

Yikes, thought Horrid Henry. What am

I going to do now? The moment he'd been dreading for weeks had arrived.

'Henry! I'm not going to ask you again,' said Mum. 'Have you finished wrapping all your Christmas presents?'

'Yes!' bellowed Horrid Henry.

This was not entirely true. Henry had not finished wrapping his Christmas presents. In fact, he hadn't even started. The truth was, Henry had finished wrapping because he had no presents to wrap.

This was certainly *not* his fault. He *had* bought a few gifts, certainly. He knew Peter would love the box of green Day-Glo slime. And if he didn't, well, he knew who to give it to. And Granny and Grandpa and Mum and Dad and Paul and Polly would have adored the big boxes of chocolates Henry had won at the school fair. Could he help it if the chocolates had called his name so loudly that he'd

been forced to eat them all? And then
Granny had been complaining about
gaining weight. Surely it would have
been very unkind to give her chocolate.
And eating chocolate would have just
made Pimply Paul's pimples worse.
Henry'd done him a big favour eating
that box.

And it was hardly Henry's fault when
he'd needed extra goo for a raid on the
Secret Club and Peter's present was the
only stuff to hand. He'd *meant* to buy
replacements. But he had so many things
he needed to buy for himself that when
he opened his skeleton bank to get out
some cash for Christmas shopping, only
35p had rolled out.

'I've bought and wrapped all *my*
presents, Mum,' said Perfect Peter. 'I've
been saving my pocket money for
months.'

'Whoopee for you,' said Henry.

'Henry, it's always better to give than to receive,' said Peter.

Mum beamed. 'Quite right, Peter.'

'Says who?' growled Horrid Henry. 'I'd much rather *get* presents.'

'Don't be so horrid, Henry,' said Mum.

'Don't be so selfish, Henry,' said Dad.

Horrid Henry stuck out his tongue.
Mum and Dad gasped.

'You horrid boy,' said Mum.

'I just hope Father Christmas didn't see that,' said Dad.

'Henry,' said Peter, 'Father Christmas

33

won't bring you any presents if you're bad.'

AAARRRGGHHH! Horrid Henry sprang at Peter. He was a grizzly bear guzzling a juicy morsel.

'AAAAIIEEE,' wailed Peter. 'Henry pinched me.'

'Henry! Go to your room,' said Mum.

'Fine!' screamed Horrid Henry, stomping off and slamming the door. Why did he get stuck with the world's meanest and most horrible parents? *They* certainly didn't deserve any presents.

Presents! Why couldn't he just *get*

them? Why oh why did he have to *give*
them? Giving other people presents was
such a waste of his hard-earned money.
Every time he gave a present it meant
something he couldn't buy for himself.
Goodbye chocolate. Goodbye comics.
Goodbye Deluxe Goo-Shooter. And
then, if you bought anything good, it was
so horrible having to give it away. He'd
practically cried having to give Ralph
that Terminator Gladiator poster for his
birthday. And the Mutant Max lunchbox
Mum made him give Kasim still made
him gnash his teeth whenever he saw
Kasim with it.

Now he was stuck, on Christmas
Eve, with no money, and no presents to
give anyone, deserving or not.

And then Henry had a wonderful,
spectacular idea. It was so wonderful,
and so spectacular, that he couldn't
believe he hadn't thought of it before.

Who said he had to *buy* presents? Didn't
Mum and Dad always say it was the
thought that counted? And oh boy was
he thinking.

Granny was sure to love a Mutant
Max comic. After all, who wouldn't?
Then when she'd finished enjoying it,
he could borrow it back. Horrid Henry
rummaged under his bed and found a
recent copy. In fact, it would be a shame
if Grandpa got jealous of Granny's great
present. Safer to give them each one,
thought Henry, digging deep into his
pile to find one with the fewest torn
pages.

Now let's see, Mum and Dad. He
could draw them a lovely picture. Nah,
that would take too long. Even better,
he could write them a poem.

Henry sat down at his desk, grabbed
a pencil, and wrote:

36

Dear Old baldy Dad
Don't be sad
Be glad
Because you've had...
A very merry Christmas
Love from your lad,
Henry

Not bad, thought Henry. Not bad. And so cheap! Now one for Mum.

Dear Old wrinkly Mum
Don't be glum
Cause you've got a fat tum
And an even bigger bum
Ho ho ho hum
Love from your son,

Henry

Wow! It was hard finding so many
words to rhyme with *mum* but he'd done
it. And the poem was nice and Christmasy
with the 'ho ho ho'. *Son* didn't rhyme
but hopefully Mum wouldn't notice

because she'd be so thrilled with the rest of the poem. When he was famous she'd be proud to show off the poem her son had written specially for her.

Now, Polly. Hmmmn. She was always squeaking and squealing about dirt and dust. Maybe a lovely kitchen sponge? Or a rag she could use to mop up after Vera? Or a bucket to put over Pimply Paul's head?

Wait. What about some soap?

Horrid Henry nipped into the bathroom. Yes! There was a tempting bar of blue soap going to waste in the soap dish by the bathtub. True, it had been used once or twice, but a bit of smoothing with his fingers would sort that out. In fact, Polly and Paul could share this present, it was such a good one.

Whistling, Horrid Henry wrapped up the soap in sparkling reindeer paper. He was a genius. Why hadn't he ever done this before? And a lovely rag from under the sink would be perfect as a gag for Vera.

That just left Peter and all his present problems would be over. A piece of chewing gum, only one careful owner? A collage of sweet wrappers which spelled out *Worm*? The unused comb Peter had given *him* last Christmas?

Aha. Peter loved bunnies. What better present than a picture of a bunny?

It was the work of a few moments for Henry to draw a bunny and slash a few blue lines across it to colour it in. Then he signed his name in big

letters at the bottom. Maybe he should
be a famous artist and not a poet when
he grew up, he thought, admiring his
handiwork. Henry had heard that artists
got paid loads of cash just for stacking a
few bricks or hurling paint at a white
canvas. Being an artist sounded like a
great job, since it left so much time for
playing computer games.

Horrid Henry dumped his presents
beneath the Christmas tree and sighed
happily. This was one Christmas where he
was sure to get a lot more than he gave.
Whoopee! Who could ask for anything
more?

HORRID HENRY'S AMBUSH

Christmas Eve
(just a few more hours to go!)

It was Christmas Eve at last. Every minute felt like an hour. Every hour felt like a year. How could Henry live until Christmas morning when he could get his hands on all his loot?

Mum and Dad were baking frantically in the kitchen.

Perfect Peter sat by the twinkling Christmas tree scratching out 'Silent Night' over and over again on his cello.

43

'Can't you play something else?' snapped Henry.

'No,' said Peter, sawing away. 'This is the only Christmas carol I know. You can move if you don't like it.'

'You move,' said Henry.

Peter ignored him.

'Siiiiiiiiii—lent Niiiiight,' screeched the cello.

AAARRRGH.

Horrid Henry lay on the sofa with his fingers in his ears, double-checking his choices from the Toy Heaven catalogue. Big red 'X's' appeared on every page, to help you-know-who remember all the toys he absolutely had to have. Oh please, let everything he wanted leap from its pages and into Santa's sack. After all, what could be better than looking at a huge glittering stack of presents on Christmas morning, and knowing that they were all for you?

Oh please let this be the year when he finally got everything he wanted!

His letter to Father Christmas couldn't have been clearer.

Dear Father Christmas,

I want loads and loads and loads of cash, to make up for the puny amount you put in my stocking last year. And a Robomatic Supersonic Space Howler Deluxe plus attachments would be great, too. I have asked for this before, you know!!! And the Terminator Gladiator fighting kit. I need lots more Day-Glo slime and comics and a Mutant Max poster and the new Zapatron Hip-Hop Dinosaur. This is your last chance.

Henry

PS. Satsumas are NOT presents!!!!!
PPS. Peter asked me to tell you to give me all his presents as he doesn't want any.

How hard could it be for Father Christmas to get this right? He'd asked for the Space Howler last year, and it never arrived. Instead, Henry got . . . vests. And handkerchiefs. And books. And clothes. And a—bleuccccck—jigsaw puzzle and a skipping rope and a tiny supersoaker instead of the mega-sized one he'd specified. Yuck! Father Christmas obviously needed Henry's help.

Father Christmas is getting old and doddery, thought Henry. Maybe he hasn't got my letters. Maybe he's lost his reading glasses. Or—what a horrible thought—

maybe he was delivering Henry's presents
by mistake to some other Henry. Eeeek!
Some yucky, undeserving Henry was
probably right now this minute playing
with Henry's Terminator Gladiator sword,
shield, axe, and trident. And enjoying his
Intergalactic Samurai Gorillas. It was so
unfair!

And then suddenly Henry had a
brilliant, spectacular idea. Why had he
never thought of this before? All his
present problems would be over. Presents
were far too important to leave to Father
Christmas. Since he couldn't be trusted
to bring the right gifts, Horrid Henry had
no choice. He would have to ambush
Father Christmas.

Yes!

He'd hold Father Christmas hostage
with his Goo-Shooter, while he rummaged
in his present sack for all the loot he was
owed. Maybe Henry would keep the lot.

Now *that* would be fair.

Let's see, thought Horrid Henry. Father Christmas was bound to be a slippery character, so he'd need to booby-trap his bedroom. When you-know-who sneaked in to fill his stocking at the end of the bed, Henry could leap up and nab him. Father Christmas had a lot of explaining to do for all those years of stockings filled with satsumas and walnuts instead of chocolate and cold hard cash.

So, how best to capture him?

Henry considered.

A bucket of water above the door.

A skipping rope stretched tight across the entrance, guaranteed to trip up intruders.

A web of string criss-crossed from bedpost to door and threaded with bells to ensnare night-time visitors.

And let's not forget strategically scattered whoopee cushions.

His plan was foolproof.

Loot, here I come, thought Horrid Henry.

Horrid Henry sat up in bed, his Goo-Shooter aimed at the half-open door

49

where a bucket of water balanced. All his traps were laid. No one was getting in without Henry knowing about it. Any minute now, he'd catch Father Christmas and make him pay up.

Henry waited. And waited. And waited. His eyes started to feel heavy and he closed them for a moment.

There was a rustling at Henry's door.

Oh my god, this was it! Henry lay down and pretended to be asleep.

Cr-eeeek.

Cr-eeeek.

Horrid Henry reached for his Goo-Shooter.

A huge shape loomed in the doorway.

Henry braced himself to attack.

'Doesn't he look sweet when he's asleep?' whispered the shape.

'What a little snugglechops,' whispered another.

Sweet? Snugglechops?

Horrid Henry's fingers itched to let Mum and Dad have it with both barrels.

POW!

Splat!

Henry could see it now. Mum covered in green goo. Dad covered in green goo. Mum and Dad snatching the Goo-Shooter and wrecking all his plans and throwing out all his presents and banning him from TV for ever . . . hmmmn. His fingers felt a little less itchy.

Henry lowered his Goo-Shooter. The bucket of water wobbled above the door.

Yikes! What if Mum and Dad stepped into his Santa traps? All his hard work—ruined.

'I'm awake,' snarled Henry.

The shapes stepped back. The water stopped wobbling.

'Go to sleep!' hissed Mum.

'Go to sleep!' hissed Dad.

'What are you doing here?' demanded Henry.

'Checking on you,' said Mum. 'Now go to sleep or Father Christmas will never come.'

He'd better, thought Henry.

Horrid Henry woke with a jolt. AAARRGGH! He'd fallen asleep. How could he? Panting and gasping Henry switched on the light. Phew. His traps were intact. His stocking was empty. Father Christmas hadn't been yet.

Wow, was that lucky. That was incredibly lucky. Henry lay back, his heart pounding.

And then Horrid Henry had a terrible thought.

What if Father Christmas had decided to be spiteful and *avoid* Henry's bedroom this year? Or what if he'd played a sneaky trick on Henry and filled a stocking *downstairs* instead?

Nah. No way.

But wait. When Father Christmas came to Rude Ralph's house he always filled the stockings downstairs. Now Henry came to think of it, Moody Margaret always left her stocking downstairs too, hanging from the fireplace, not from the end of her bed, like Henry did.

Horrid Henry looked at the clock. It

was past midnight. Mum and Dad had forbidden him to go downstairs till morning, on pain of having all his presents taken away and no telly all day.

But this was an emergency. He'd creep downstairs, take a quick peek to make sure he hadn't missed Father Christmas, then be back in bed in a jiffy.

No one will ever know, thought Horrid Henry.

Henry tiptoed round the whoopee cushions, leaped over the criss-cross threads, stepped over the skipping rope and carefully squeezed through his door so as not to disturb the bucket of water. Then he crept downstairs.

Sneak
   Sneak
      Sneak

Horrid Henry shone his torch over the sitting room. Father Christmas hadn't been. The room was exactly as he'd left it that evening.

Except for one thing. Henry's light illuminated the Christmas tree, heavy with chocolate santas and chocolate bells and chocolate reindeer. Mum and Dad must have hung them on the tree after he'd gone to bed.

Horrid Henry looked at the chocolates cluttering up the Christmas tree. Shame, thought Horrid Henry, the way those chocolates spoil the view of all those lovely decorations. You could barely see the baubles and tinsel he and Peter had worked so hard to put on.

'Hi, Henry,' said the chocolate santas. 'Don't you want to eat us?'

'Go on, Henry,' said the chocolate bells.

'You know you want to.'

'What are you waiting for, Henry?' urged the chocolate reindeer.

What indeed? After all, it *was* Christmas.

Henry took a chocolate santa or three from the side, and then another two from the back. Hmmn, boy, was that great chocolate, he thought, stuffing them into his mouth.

Oops. Now the chocolate santas looked a little unbalanced.

Better take a few from the front and from the other side, to even it up, thought Henry. Then no one will notice there are a few chocolates missing.

Henry gobbled and gorged and guzzled. Wow, were those chocolates yummy!!!

The tree looks a bit bare, thought Henry a little while later. Mum had such eagle eyes she might notice that a few— well, all—of the chocolates were missing. He'd better hide all those gaps with a

few extra baubles. And, while he was
improving the tree, he could swap that
stupid fairy for Terminator Gladiator.

Henry piled extra decorations onto the
branches. Soon the Christmas tree was
so covered in baubles and tinsel there
was barely a hint of green. No one
would notice the missing chocolates.
Then Henry stood on a chair, dumped
the fairy, and, standing on his tippy-tippy
toes, hung Terminator Gladiator at the
top where he belonged.

Perfect, thought Horrid Henry, jumping off the chair and stepping back to admire his work. Absolutely perfect. Thanks to me this is the best tree ever.

There was a terrible creaking sound. Then another. Then suddenly . . .

CRASH!

58

The Christmas tree toppled over.

Horrid Henry's heart stopped.

Upstairs he could hear Mum and Dad stirring.

'Oy! Who's down there?' shouted Dad.

RUN!!! thought Horrid Henry. Run for your life!!

Horrid Henry ran like he had never run before, up the stairs to his room before Mum and Dad could catch him. Oh please let him get there in time. His parents' bedroom door opened just as Henry dashed inside his room. He'd made it. He was safe.

SPLASH! The bucket of water spilled all over him.

TRIP! Horrid Henry fell over the skipping rope.

CRASH! SMASH! RING! RING! jangled the bells.

PLLLLLLL! belched the whoopee cushions.

'What is going on in here?' shrieked Mum, glaring.

'Nothing,' said Horrid Henry, as he lay sprawled on the floor soaking wet and tangled up in threads and wires and rope. 'I heard a noise downstairs so I got up to check,' he added innocently.

'Tree's fallen over,' called Dad. 'Must have been overloaded. Don't worry, I'll sort it.'

'Get back to bed, Henry,' said Mum wearily. 'And don't touch your stocking till morning.'

Henry looked. And gasped. His stocking was stuffed and bulging. That mean old sneak, thought Horrid Henry indignantly. How did he do it? How had he escaped the traps?

Watch out Father Christmas, thought Horrid Henry. I'll get you next year.

4

HORRID HENRY'S CHRISTMAS LUNCH

25 December (at last!)

'Oh, handkerchiefs, just what I wanted,' said Perfect Peter. 'Thank you *so* much.'

'Not handkerchiefs *again*,' moaned Horrid Henry, throwing the hankies aside and ripping the paper off the next present in his pile.

'Don't tear the wrapping paper!' squeaked Perfect Peter.

Horrid Henry ripped open the present and groaned.

Yuck (a pen, pencil, and ruler). Yuck (a dictionary). Yuck (gloves). OK (£15— should have been a lot more). Eeew (a pink bow tie from Aunt Ruby). Eeew (mints). Yum (huge tin of chocolates). Good (five more knights for his army). Very good (a subscription to Gross-Out Fan Club) . . .

And (very very good) a Terminator Gladiator trident . . . and . . .

And . . . where was the rest?

'Is that it?' shrieked Henry.

'You haven't opened my present, Henry,' said Peter. 'I hope you like it.'

Horrid Henry tore off the wrapping. It was a Manners With Maggie calendar.

'Ugh, gross,' said Henry. 'No thank you.'

'Henry!' said Mum. 'That's no way to receive a present.'

'I don't care,' moaned Horrid Henry. 'Where's my Zapatron Hip-Hop dinosaur? And where's the rest of the Terminator Gladiator fighting kit? I wanted everything, not just the trident.'

'Maybe next year,' said Mum.

'But I want it now!' howled Henry.

'Henry, you know that "I want doesn't get",' said Peter. 'Isn't that right, Mum?'

'It certainly is,' said Mum. 'And I haven't heard you say thank you, Henry.'

Horrid Henry glared at Peter and sprang. He was a hornet stinging a worm to death.

'WAAAAAAH!' wailed Peter.

'Henry! Stop it or—'

Ding! Dong!

'They're here!' shouted Horrid Henry, leaping up and abandoning his prey. 'That means more presents!'

'Wait, Henry,' said Mum.

But too late. Henry raced to the door and flung it open.

There stood Granny and Grandpa, Prissy Polly, Pimply Paul, and Vomiting Vera.

'Gimme my presents!' he shrieked, snatching a bag of brightly wrapped gifts out of Granny's hand and spilling them on the floor. Now, where were the ones with his name on?

'Merry Christmas, everyone,' said Mum brightly. 'Henry, don't be rude.'

'I'm not being rude,' said Henry. 'I just

want my presents. Great, money!' said
Henry, beaming. 'Thanks, Granny! But
couldn't you add a few pounds and—'

'Henry, don't be horrid!' snapped Dad.

'Let the guests take off their coats,' said
Mum.

'Bleeeeech,' said Vomiting Vera, throwing
up on Paul.

'Eeeeek,' said Polly.

All the grown-ups gathered in the sitting
room to open their gifts.

'Peter, thank you so much for the
perfume, it's my favourite,' said Granny.

'I know,' said Peter.

'And what a lovely comic,
Henry,' said Granny.
'Mutant Max is my ...
um ... favourite.'

'Thank you,
Henry,' said
Grandpa. 'This
comic looks very
... interesting.'

'I'll have it back
when you've
finished with it,' said Henry.

'Henry!' said Mum, glaring.

For some reason Polly didn't look
delighted with her present.

'Eeeek!' squeaked
Polly. 'This soap
has ... hairs in
it.' She pulled
out a long
black one.
'That came

free,' said Horrid Henry.

'We're getting you toothpaste next year, you little brat,' muttered Pimply Paul under his breath.

Honestly, there was no pleasing some people, thought Horrid Henry indignantly. He'd given Paul a great bar of soap, and he didn't seem thrilled. So much for it's the thought that counts.

'A poem,' said Mum. 'Henry, how lovely.'

'Read it out loud,' said Grandpa.

'Dear old wrinkly Mum
Don't be glum
'Cause you've got a fat tum
And an even bigger...'

'Maybe later,' said Mum.
'Another poem,' said Dad. 'Great!'
'Let's hear it,' said Granny.

'Dear old baldy Dad—

. . . and so forth,' said Dad, folding Henry's poem quickly.

'Oh,' said Polly, staring at the crystal frog vase Mum and Dad had given her.

'How funny. This looks just like the vase *I* gave Aunt Ruby for Christmas last year.'

'What a coincidence,' said Mum, blushing bright red.

'Great minds think alike,' said Dad quickly.

Dad gave Mum an iron.

'Oh, an iron, just what
I always wanted,'
said Mum.

Mum gave Dad
oven gloves.

'Oh, oven gloves,
just what I always
wanted,' said Dad.

Pimply Paul
gave Prissy Polly a
huge power drill.
'Eeeek,' squealed
Polly. 'What's this?'
'Oh, that's the
Megawatt Superduper
Drill-o-matic 670
XM3,' said Paul, 'and just wait till you see
the attachments. You're getting those for
your birthday.'

'Oh,' said Polly.

71

Granny gave Grandpa a lovely mug to put his false teeth in.

Grandpa gave Granny a shower cap and a bumper pack of dusters.

'What super presents!' said Mum.

'Yes,' said Perfect Peter. 'I loved every single one of my presents, especially the satsumas and walnuts in my stocking.'

'I didn't,' said Horrid Henry.

'Henry, don't be horrid,' said Dad. 'Who'd like a mince pie?'

'Are they homemade or from the shop?' asked Henry.

'Homemade of course,' said Dad.

'Gross,' said Henry.

'Ooh,' said Polly. 'No, Vera!' she squealed as Vera vomited all over the plate.

'Never mind,' said Mum tightly. 'There's more in the kitchen.'

Horrid Henry was bored. Horrid Henry was fed up. The presents had all been opened. His parents had made him go on a long, boring walk. Dad had confiscated his Terminator trident when he had speared Peter with it.

So, what now?

Grandpa was sitting in the armchair with his pipe, snoring, his tinsel crown slipping over his face.

Prissy Polly and Pimply Paul were squabbling over whose turn it was to change Vera's stinky nappy.

'Eeeek,' said Polly. 'I did it last.'

'I did,' said Paul.

'WAAAAAAAAA!' wailed Vomiting Vera.

Perfect Peter was watching Sammy the Snail slithering about on TV.

Horrid Henry snatched the clicker and switched channels.

'Hey, I was watching that!' protested Peter.

'Tough,' said Henry.

Let's see, what was on? 'Tra la la la ...' Ick! Daffy and her Dancing Daisies.

'Wait! I want to watch!' wailed Peter.

74

Click. ' . . . and the tension builds as the judges compare tomatoes grown . . . ' Click! ' . . . wish you a Merry Christmas, we wish you . . .' Click! 'Chartres Cathedral is one of the wonders of . . . ' Click! 'HA HA HA HA HA HA HA HA.' Opera! Click! Why was there nothing good on TV? Just a baby movie about singing cars he'd seen a million times already.

'I'm bored,' moaned Henry. 'And I'm starving.' He wandered into the kitchen, which looked like a hurricane had swept through.

'When's lunch? I thought we were eating at two. I'm starving.'

'Soon,' said Mum. She looked a little

frazzled. 'There's been a little problem
with the oven.'

'So when's lunch?' bellowed Horrid
Henry.

'When it's ready!' bellowed Dad.

Henry waited. And waited. And waited.

'When's lunch?' asked Polly.

'When's lunch?' asked Paul.

'When's lunch?' asked Peter.

'As soon as the turkey is cooked,' said
Dad. He peeked into the oven. He poked
the turkey. Then he went pale.

'It's hardly cooked,' he whispered.

'Check the temperature,' said Granny.
Dad checked.

'Oops,' said Dad.

'Never mind, we can start with the
sprouts,' said Mum cheerfully.

'That's not the right way to do sprouts,'
said Granny. 'You're peeling too many of
the leaves off.'

'Yes, Mother,' said Dad.

'That's not the right way to make bread sauce,' said Granny.

'Yes, Mother,' said Dad.

'That's not the right way to make stuffing,' said Granny.

'Yes, Mother,' said Dad.

'That's not the right way to roast potatoes,' said Granny.

'Mother!' yelped Dad. 'Leave me alone!'

'Don't be horrid,' said Granny.

'I'm not being horrid,' said Dad.

'Come along Granny, let's get you a nice drink and leave the chef on his own,' said Mum, steering Granny firmly towards the sitting room. Then she stopped.

'Is something burning?' asked Mum, sniffing.

Dad checked the oven.

'Not in here.'

There was a shriek from the sitting room.

'It's Grandpa!' shouted Perfect Peter.

Everyone ran in.

There was Grandpa, asleep in his chair. A thin column of black smoke rose from the arms. His paper crown, drooping over his pipe, was smoking.

'Whh..whh?' mumbled Grandpa, as Mum whacked him with her broom. 'AAARRGH!' he gurgled as Dad threw water over him.

'When's lunch?' screamed Horrid Henry.

'When it's ready,' screamed Dad.

★

It was dark when Henry's family finally sat down to Christmas lunch. Henry's tummy was rumbling so loudly with hunger he thought the walls would cave in. Henry and Peter made a dash to grab the seat against the wall, furthest from the kitchen.

'Get off!' shouted Henry.

'It's my turn to sit here,' wailed Peter.

'Mine!'

'Mine!'

Slap!

Slap!

'WAAAAAAAAAAA!' screeched Henry.

'WAAAAAAAAAAAA!' wailed Peter.

'Quiet!' screamed Dad.

Mum brought in fresh holly and ivy to decorate the table.

'Lovely,' said Mum, placing the boughs all along the centre.

'Very festive,' said Granny.

'I'm starving!' wailed Horrid Henry. 'This isn't Christmas lunch, it's Christmas dinner.'

'Shhh,' said Grandpa.

The turkey was finally cooked. There were platefuls of stuffing, sprouts, cranberries, bread sauce and peas.

'Smells good,' said Granny.

'Hmmn, boy,' said Grandpa. 'What a feast.'

Horrid Henry was so hungry he could eat the tablecloth.

'Come on, let's eat!' he said.

'Hold on, I'll just get the roast potatoes,' said Dad. Wearing his new oven gloves, he carried in the steaming hot potatoes in a glass roasting dish, and set it in the middle of the table.

'*Voila!*' said Dad. 'Now, who wants dark meat and who . . .'

'What's that crawling . . . aaaarrrghh!' screamed Polly. 'There are spiders every-where!'

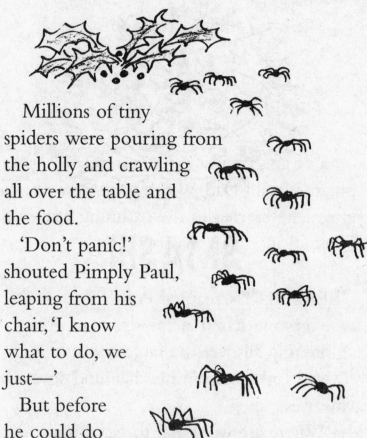

Millions of tiny spiders were pouring from the holly and crawling all over the table and the food.

'Don't panic!' shouted Pimply Paul, leaping from his chair, 'I know what to do, we just—'

But before he could do anything the glass dish with the roast potatoes exploded.

CRASH!

SMASH!

'EEEEEKK!' screamed Polly.

Everyone stared at the slivers of glass glistening all over the table and the food.

Dad sank down in his chair and covered his eyes.

'Where are we going to get more food?' whispered Mum.

'I don't know,' muttered Dad.

'I know,' said Horrid Henry, 'let's start with Christmas pudding and defrost some pizzas.'

Dad opened his eyes.

Mum opened her eyes.

'That,' said Dad, 'is a brilliant idea.'

'I really fancy some pizza,' said Grandpa.

'Me too,' said Granny.

Henry beamed. It wasn't often his ideas were recognised for their brilliance.

'Merry Christmas everyone,' said Horrid Henry. 'Merry Christmas.'

Acknowledgements

My thanks to Susie Boyt, Amanda
Craig, Judith Elliott, Fiona Kennedy
and Kate Saunders for sharing their
Christmas disaster stories
with me.

HORRID HENRY BOOKS

Horrid Factbooks

Horrid Henry's Animals
Horrid Henry's Bodies
Horrid Henry's Bugs
Horrid Henry's Crazy Creatures
Horrid Henry's Dinosaurs
Horrid Henry's Food
Horrid Henry's Ghosts
Horrid Henry's Kings and Queens
Horrid Henry's Sports

Joke Books

Horrid Henry's Joke Book
Horrid Henry's Jolly Joke Book
Horrid Henry's Mighty Joke Book
Horrid Henry's Hilariously Horrid Joke Book
Horrid Henry's Purple Hand Gang Joke Book
Horrid Henry's All Time Favourite Joke Book

Colour books

Horrid Henry's Big Bad Book
Horrid Henry's Wicked Ways
Horrid Henry's Evil Enemies
Horrid Henry Rules the World
Horrid Henry's House of Horrors
Horrid Henry's Dreadful Deeds
Horrid Henry Shows Who's Boss
Horrid Henry's Tricky Tricks

Horrid Henry's Fearsome Four